This book belongs to

....

Address ....

....

....

Age ....

Written by Brian Miles, Illustrated by Ken McKie.
Text©1989 Brian Miles, illustrations©Grandreams Limited.

Published by
Grandreams Limited,
Jadwin House, 205/211 Kentish Town Road,
London, NW5 2JU.

Printed in Czechoslovakia.

ISBN 0 86227 721 3

KM35-36

Teddy Tales in this book:

TEDDY
Takes a Train

Teddy was sitting aloft, high in his favourite tree,
　　　Enjoying a pot of honey, for his afternoon tea.
Suddenly from far below, he heard a cheerful cry,
　　　It was Jimbo, Bessy and Belle who were walking by.

Teddy quickly swung down
    to greet his good friends the bears.
Then all sat down together,
    using logs for chairs.
Teddy Bear said: "I've been thinking.
    About all sorts of things today.
And I've had a good idea,
    for a trip on a train away-day."

"What a very good idea." They all at once agreed,
    "Yes, a trip on a train, would be very nice indeed."
Bessy and Belle exclaimed, "But wherever shall we go?"
    "To Teddy Town," said Teddy, "it's really nice you know."

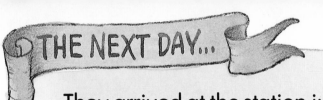

They arrived at the station just before eight,
The bears all hoping their train would not be late.
They waited and listened to hear the train whistle: "Hello."
Then it puffed into the station—what a magnificent show!

The engine was painted, in a bright red and green,
        There was black smoke puffing and a hissing of steam.
The engine huffed, puffed and snorted with impatient glee,
        As it pulled six green carriages up to platform three.

The bears with tickets ready, stepped up on board,
      The carriage doors banged shut, then the engine roared.
CLICKETY-CLICK, CLICKETY-CLACK THE TRAIN WENT
      CHUGGING DOWN THE TRACK.
Woo-Woo whistled the train as it sped on its way,
      Teddy clapped paws and whooped: "Oh what a lovely day."

The train rattled along speeding over the rails,
Past villages and farms, over hills and
through dales.
At last in high spirits, they arrived at
Teddy Town Station,
And alighted on the platform,
with great anticipation.

They went to the museum, of Ancient Bear Art,
where they saw a nice picture, of an ox and a cart.
It was by Constable Bear, and was called "The Haywain".
Bessy said,"It's beautiful, we must come here again."

Then they went to the zoo,
　　　to see the animals there,
There were lots of friendly creatures and some
　　　were quite rare.
They bought some postcards, of their friends
　　　in the zoo.
And Teddy then sent one, to Winnie the Pooh!

At lunch time Jimbo said, "I'm ready to eat,"
    So they bought some ice-creams, as a special treat.
They each had a choc-bar, with nuts on the top,
    Then each had a glass, of orange fizzy-pop!

The bears then decided
        they would go to the fair,
Where they each bought a balloon
        from nice Grizzly Bear.
Jimbo chose a red one,
        Teddy chose a blue,
Bessy chose a pink one
        and so did Belle too.

They went on the dodgems and then on a big slide,
Then hurtled all around on a moon rocket ride.

They went on the big wheel high above the ground,
Then on the big dipper which went all around.

Then on to the hoop-la,
for prizes to win,
Jimbo threw first,
and won a lovely cake tin.

Bessy won a ball,
Teddy won a bat,
And Belle won a big
red feathery hat!

The Bears went on the ghost train,
  Then into the haunted house,
Belle screamed at the top of her voice,
  when she saw a little field mouse.
He said his name was Fred and
  he had been living there a year.
He was dining off some cheese
  and the very best ginger-beer.

But now the bears were hungry
and the time was getting late,
"Let's have a nice fish and chip supper.
Not in the paper, but on a plate."
So they went to the Sea-Shell restaurant,
the nicest one in town.
Where they had a feast of fish and chips,
with tea to wash it down.

And thus fortified the bears set forth,
      Their homeward train to catch.
Jimbo gave his balloon to Belle,
      Her feathery hat to match.

As they neared the station happily, they saw
their friends from school.
There were David, Katy and Lucy and Joshua
and Saul!
They boarded the train at six-thirty, sitting
together inside.
The sun was sinking slowly, as in the train
they began to ride.

They arrived back home so happy
and without any worries or cares.
Their Mummies and Daddies were waiting
for the tired little Teddy Bears.

TEDDY
and
The Flying Circus

Teddy gazed up at a sky of clear blue,
At a silver speck coming into view.
The speck began to hum like a bumblebee,
Then began to fall like a leaf from a tree.

The tiny speck grew larger and Teddy could see,
A glittering aeroplane with a bright red 'B'.
The plane flashed low just above the trees,
Causing branches to dance in the breeze.

Then it soared up high into the blue,
        Trailing vapour as upwards it flew.
It dived and looped the loop, banked and spun,
        Yellow wings glittering in the sun.

Then flying slowly
        The plane dived low,
"Golly," thought Teddy,
        "what a great show."
Beaming from the cockpit
        And after looking all around,
The pilot brought his gleaming
        Machine, safely to the ground.

The pilot stepped down from his cockpit
        and said, "Hello, you young bear,
my name is Captain Bogglesworth
        and I've just come from over there.
I lead a flying circus and I'm looking
        for a place without hills,
where we can put on a flying display
        and demonstrate all our skills."

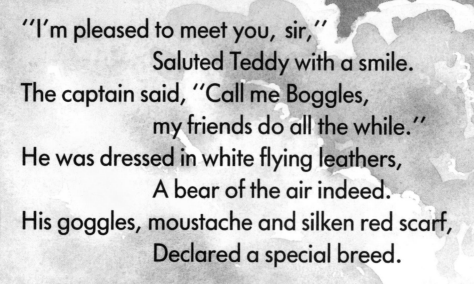

"I'm pleased to meet you, sir,"
　　　　Saluted Teddy with a smile.
The captain said, "Call me Boggles,
　　　　my friends do all the while."
He was dressed in white flying leathers,
　　　　A bear of the air indeed.
His goggles, moustache and silken red scarf,
　　　　Declared a special breed.

Teddy was very excited and said,
          "Do you think that this field will do?"
"It looks perfect to me," said Boggles,
          "but I must fetch the rest
of the crew."

He climbed back into the cockpit.
          And soon the engine spluttered
and roared,
          With a smile and a wave
to Teddy,
          He sped across the field
and soared.

Teddy rushed off to tell his friends,
About the exciting events of the day.
He told them about Captain Boggles
And his aerobatic flying display.
Jimbo said, "Wouldn't it be lovely
If we could go up in a plane."
Teddy said, "I'm sure that we can,
I'll ask when I see Boggles again."

The next morning the bears assembled,
        By the edge of the field,
They waited for signs of the aeroplanes,
        Their ears and eyes peeled.
Suddenly they heard the engines
        And the sky above them revealed,
Planes of all types and vintages
        As round and round they wheeled.

One by one they landed
   And taxied till they stopped,
Boggles waved to Teddy
   As to the ground he hopped.
He then introduced his pilots as:
   "A very daring bunch,"
Then invited Teddy and his friends
   To join them all for lunch!

Teddy was admiring Red
        Baron Bear's plane when
Boggles cried, ''Today!
        We must make our plans
for next weekend, to give
        a grand flying display.''
''A good idea!'' said Teddy.
        ''But I have something
important to say,
        can you teach me to fly
an aeroplane Boggles,
        by next Saturday?''
Boggles laughed and said,
        ''Why not?
It shouldn't take too long.
        I'll make a pilot of
you I'm sure,
        follow me and you
cannot go wrong!''

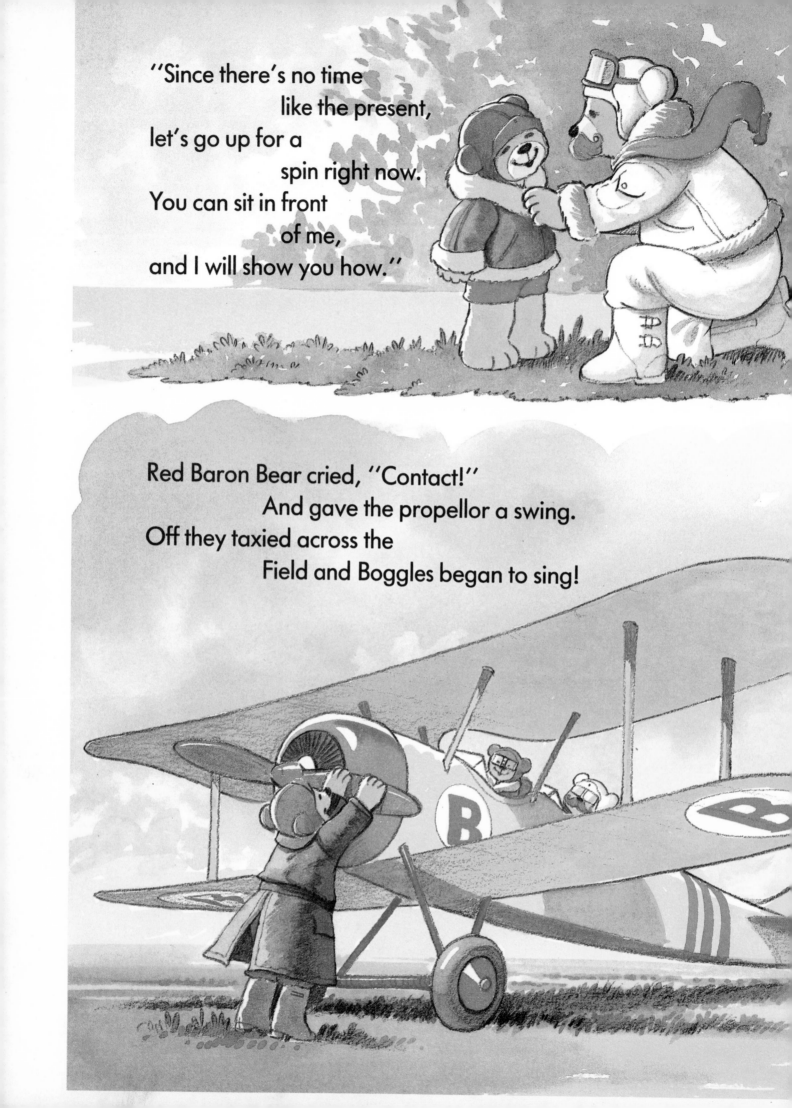

"Since there's no time
                     like the present,
let's go up for a
                     spin right now.
You can sit in front
                     of me,
and I will show you how."

Red Baron Bear cried, "Contact!"
                     And gave the propellor a swing.
Off they taxied across the
                     Field and Boggles began to sing!

Soon they were soaring
   High in the sky, climbing
With tremendous power.
   Teddy looked down at
The village church and
   Saw Vicar Bear in the tower!
Boggles said, "Now I will
   teach you to fly, it's
as simple as can be,
   just keep paying attention,
listen carefully and follow me."

Teddy followed his instructor with care
And quickly began to learn,
By moving the controls to the left or right,
The plane was made to turn.
Pushing forward the plane dived low
And pulling back the plane climbed high.

Teddy was having a marvellous time
       With Boggles in the sky.
Boggles said, ''Well done young Ted,
       now I think we'll take her down.
You have earned your wings as I knew you would
       and you'll soon be the talk of the Town.''

When the great day came
And the circus took to the air,
The Pilot bears performed
With intrepid skills so rare.
They flew daring aerobatics
For all the spectators to view,
And then with vapour trails
Streaming, etched patterns
Of red, white and blue.

Then Captain Bogglesworth announced,
"Now is the grand finale!"
It was to be performed by Teddy,
Jimbo, Belle and Bessy.

The huge crowd of bears in the grandstand,
Waited in silent awe,
Then burst into rapturous applause,
With a tremendous roar!

CAPTAIN BOGGLES
FLYING CIRCUS

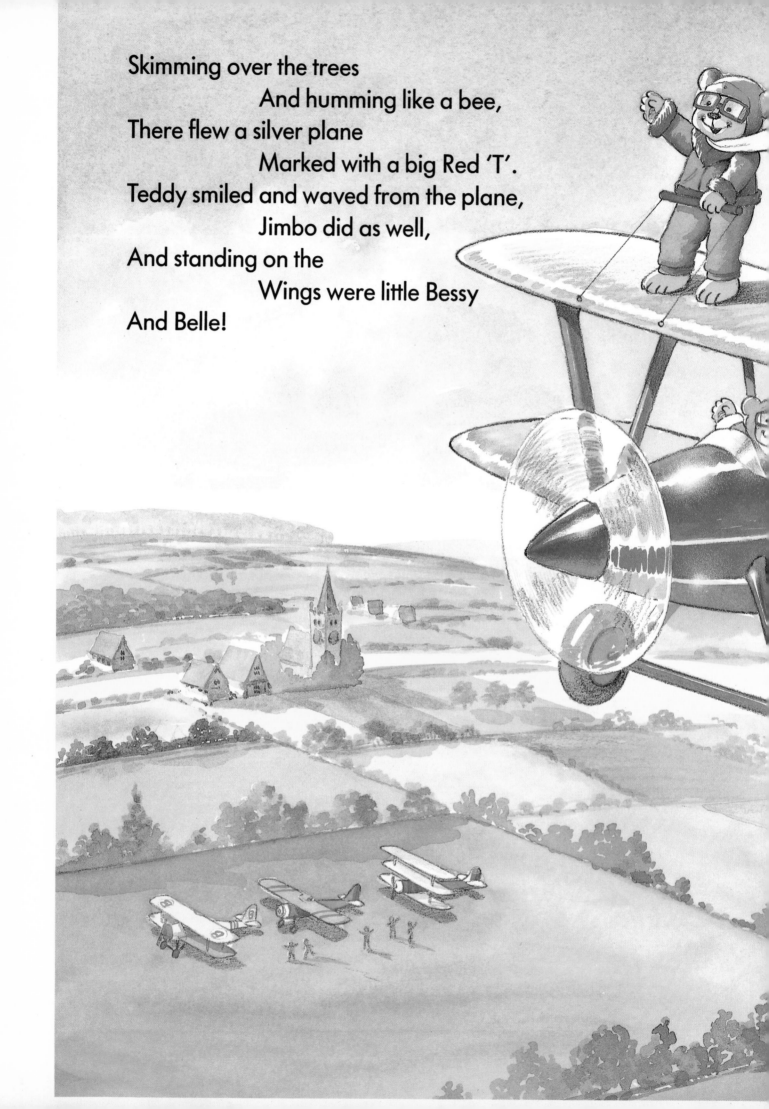

Skimming over the trees
And humming like a bee,
There flew a silver plane
Marked with a big Red 'T'.
Teddy smiled and waved from the plane,
Jimbo did as well,
And standing on the
Wings were little Bessy
And Belle!

There were claps and cheers and hats in the air,
          For their magnificent feat,
And Boggles said, "Ladies and Gentlebears,
          that was certainly a treat.
We have had a lovely time,
          entertaining you one and all,
and tonight you must come,
          to our Flying Circus farewell ball."

The Teddy Bear ball was splendid
And went off very well,
Teddy dancing with Bessy
And Jimbo dancing with Belle.
The Lord Mayor Bear made a little speech,
Recalling the daring scenes,
Of Boggles and his bears and their
Magnificent flying machines.

So that is the end of
The story, and of Teddy
Who learned how to fly.
And of Boggles and
His merry bears, and
A flying circus in the sky.
And if on a summer's day,
You should hear the hum
Of the bees,
Stand quite still, listen
carefully, and look above
The trees.

TEDDY

and
The Mystery of The Missing Milk

"All is not well," Teddy heard them all say.
"Some more milk was taken only yesterday.
Teddy Milkbear left it by the front door,
But when Mrs. Bruin looked, it was there no more."

"It's a mystery," they said, "it happens every day,
   Who can it be that steals the milk away?"
Teddy and his friends listened to the talk,
   And then quietly decided to go for a walk.

Bessy Bear said, "It's happened before,
    Only last week it disappeared from our door."
"It is very mysterious," Jimbo said.
    "Who takes the milk,
When we're all snug in bed?"

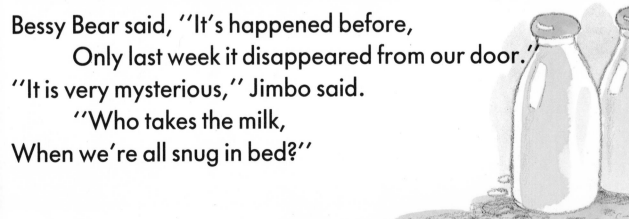

Teddy Bear said, with a solemn frown,
    "We must catch this thief of infamous renown."
"Those are big words," Jimbo declared.
    "But catch him we will, we're not scared."

Teddy Bear said, ''We must plan very hard,
    And catch the thief when he's off his guard.
Tomorrow morning, before the cock crows,
    We will get up early and see if he shows.''

Jimbo said, ''Let's meet at six,
    And like real detectives, carry walking sticks.
A walking stick is a jolly good idea,
    A magnifying glass also, will make things clear.''

As the church clock chimed six,
    The Detective Bears met.
The sun was just rising,
    And the grass was dew wet.
"Milkbear has already
    Started his round,
So let's keep our eyes peeled
    Close to the ground."

Teddy Bear led them down the village street,
    But stopped to examine some marks by a seat.
"Our thief has small feet," he said with a frown,
    Just then came a shout from Mister Bear Brown.

"My milk has gone," he cried in despair.
 And with a quizzical expression,
Scratched his bear hair.
 Jimbo said, "He can't have gone far,
After him quick, he may have a car."

Up and down the street they looked in vain,
But their eyes saw nothing, so they all looked again.
"This thief is crafty," Teddy Bear said.
"He may have small feet, but he's one step ahead!"

"Let's examine the facts," Teddy Bear said,
    "The thief must have struck when we were in bed.
Tomorrow at five, we all must meet,
    Then perhaps we can stop him having his treat."

At five the next morning,
        By the village green,
They looked all around,
        But not a soul could be seen.
Milkbear had started,
        Already that day,
And the bears followed on,
        A short distance away.

Suddenly from behind, a cry was heard,
    "Who's taken my milk?"
"Not me!" said a bird.
    A cheeky sparrow was perched in a tree,
"Call yourselves detectives?
    You couldn't catch a flea!"

Just then, Post Bear appeared delivering the mail,
  "I think your thief might have a bushy tail."
The bears asked him just what he had seen.
  With a smile, he pointed across the village green.

"Behind Grandma Bear's cottage,
    There's a cat, smooth as silk.
And I saw her this morning,
    With a bottle of milk."
The bears scampered to the cottage,
    Behind which was a shed,
And inside saw six kittens,
    All tucked up in bed.

Mother Cat was feeding them, in bed where they lay,
Tiny and snug in the sweet smelling hay.
When she first saw the bears,
She was startled at the sight,
But then told them all of her sad, sorry plight.

The kittens had been poorly,
    And needed extra food.
She knew stealing was wrong,
    But hoped they understood.
As soon as they were strong,
    They would start to repay.
By chasing all the village mice, far, far away.

The bears were happy to hear,
　　What Mother Cat had to tell,
And told her not to worry,
　　And that all would soon be well.
They would ask Milkbear to deliver,
　　A special pint for her,
And send a 'GET WELL SOON' card,
　　For the cats with silken fur.

So all has ended happily,
    The kittens are fit and well.
I hope you enjoyed this story,
    It was a tale I had to tell!

TEDDY
and
The Seaside Holiday

Teddy was happy and filled with glee,
Today, they were going to Sunbury-on-Sea.
In a cottage by the sea, they were going to stay,
This was the start of their summer holiday.

Their bags were packed with all they would need,
Including buckets, spades and books to read.
Daddy Bear started his bright red car,
And off they went, with a loud hurrah!

They had a cottage,
      With their cousins to share.
Excited and happy,
      They longed to be there.
On they drove,
      Not stopping for tea,
And at last they arrived,
      At Sunbury-on-Sea.

The other bears had only just arrived too,
And the sun shone down, from a sky of blue.
They hurriedly put their swimming costumes on,
Then off to the beach they were very soon gone.

They swam and splashed,
        In the bright shining sea,
Then dried off with towels,
        And went home for tea.

The grown-up bears had been busy indeed,
        And on brown bread and honey they began to feed.

There were fresh fruit, nuts,
    And lots to eat,
Being on holiday,
    Was certainly a treat.

Soon they were full,
    And the tired little bears,
Said, "Goodnight," to their parents,
    And went upstairs.

Each had a bed,
   In the room at the top,
After brushing their teeth,
   'Neath the sheets did hop.
Teddy and Jimbo,
   Were soon fast asleep,
But Bessy and Belle,
   To the window did creep.

They looked out upon a silvery sea,
    And there in the moonlight a tall ship did see.
It was close to the shore, and a light flashed near by,
    "Keep clear of the rocks," it seemed to cry.

Suddenly from the ship, a small boat they saw,
    Some Sailor Bears were rowing hard for the shore.
They jumped in the surf, giving each other a hand,
    Then hauled their boat up onto the sand.

They lit a fire and dried their feet,
    Then all sat down and began to eat.
They sang, "Yo ho ho, how happy are we,
    It's a good life for a bear when he's sailing the sea!"

Bessy and Belle were feeling sleepy at last,
   And looking at the clock, saw it was midnight past.
So they slipped into their nice warm beds,
   And snuggled deep down their furry heads.

At breakfast next day,
    They told what they had seen,
But Teddy and Jimbo said,
    "It might be a dream."
So they went to the beach,
    And looked at the sand.
In the remains of the fire,
    They found a gold band.

"Pirates' gold, that's what it must be,"
Said Teddy, with great authority.
They cleaned off the ash and inside did look,
And all together read, "Captain Hook."

Just as they were wondering what to do,
Bosun Bear came into view.
"I'm the keeper of the lighthouse,"
He told the bears,
"And I've just walked down,
Three hundred stairs."

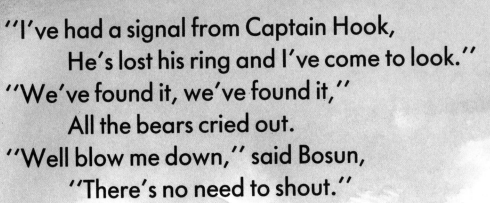

"I've had a signal from Captain Hook,
    He's lost his ring and I've come to look."
"We've found it, we've found it,"
    All the bears cried out.
"Well blow me down," said Bosun,
    "There's no need to shout."

"I'll signal the Captain in Plymouth Sound,
    He'll be very pleased that his ring has been found.
There's sure to be a reward for you young bears,
    So it's back to the lighthouse and climbing those stairs."

Captain Hook and his crew returned next day,
   They were glad they hadn't sailed too far away.
"It was careless of me to let my ring slip free.
   You must be my guests and spend a day on the sea."

The bears rushed home,
　　　Their parents to bring,
And tell them all about,
　　　Captain Hook's ring.
They sailed the sea,
　　　For the rest of the day,
Then in the evening,
　　　Returned to the bay.

Captain Hook said, "We must do this again,
    But now we're off to the Spanish Maine.
Goodbye my hearties and be of good cheer,
    I'll see you again; same time next year!"